Leap of Faith

PRAISE FOR *STORYSHARES*

"One of the brightest innovators and game-changers in the education industry."
– Forbes

"Your success in applying research-validated practices to promote literacy serves as a valuable model for other organizations seeking to create evidence-based literacy programs."
- Library of Congress

"We need powerful social and educational innovation, and Storyshares is breaking new ground. The organization addresses critical problems facing our students and teachers. I am excited about the strategies it brings to the collective work of making sure every student has an equal chance in life."
– Teach For America

"Around the world, this is one of the up-and-coming trailblazers changing the landscape of literacy and education."
- International Literacy Association

"It's the perfect idea. There's really nothing like this. I mean wow, this will be a wonderful experience for young people."   - Andrea Davis Pinkney, Executive Director, Scholastic

"Reading for meaning opens opportunities for a lifetime of learning. Providing emerging readers with engaging texts that are designed to offer both challenges and support for each individual will improve their lives for years to come. Storyshares is a wonderful start."
- David Rose, Co-founder of CAST & UDL

Leap of Faith

Angela Dellisola

STORYSHARES

Story Share, Inc.
New York. Boston. Philadelphia

Copyright © 2022 Angela Dellisola

All rights reserved.

Published in the United States by Story Share, Inc.

The characters and events in this book are fictitious. Any similarity to real persons, living or dead, is entirely coincidental.

Storyshares
Story Share, Inc.
24 N. Bryn Mawr Avenue #340
Bryn Mawr, PA 19010-3304
www.storyshares.org

Inspiring reading with a new kind of book.

Interest Level: High School
Grade Level Equivalent: 2.8

9781642611236

Book design by Storyshares

Printed in the United States of America

Storyshares Presents

1

I sat at the back of the classroom, arms folded over my chest. I hated days like today. There was nothing wrong with me.

Put anyone else in my shoes and ask them what they wanted. I'm sure they would tell you the same thing. To never, *ever* do that again. I shook my head quickly to clear the memories. No point in keeping them. No point in making more.

"Eleanor!" Mr. Tarniby barked, hitting his fist on the table. I can't help you if you don't listen to me!

"I never asked for help," I answered sharply. It was true. None of this was my idea.

"You don't want to train anymore," he said. It was the same argument every time.

"I didn't know what it was like," I told him. That's the truth. I never knew how bad it could hurt to lose someone. Someone you cared about. Someone you loved.

The problem was that no one knew what really happened. No one knew where I went. No one knew how I got so off track. And no one knew about Chase.

"You spent two years traveling, Eleanor," Mr. Tarniby said. I hated the way he said my name.

I really hated my name, period.

And I definitely hated our sessions in the dusty, unused classroom. "From what I have been told, you really enjoyed it," he said.

"Traveling through time is just like traveling our world," I insisted. "Some places rock. Some places suck."

"Watch your language," he warned, his forehead growing sweaty. "Look. I can understand it must have been scary to fall so far off track. And it took a long time to find you. That's true. But you have a gift, Eleanor. A rare gift. How can you be willing to give that up so easily?"

I looked over at the clock and almost smiled. Five minutes left. The problem was, he would keep me all day if he had to. It was a pretty big deal to refuse the "gift."

I rolled my eyes. "I don't know what you want me to say," I lied. I felt my chest getting tight and my head was pounding. "If you want me to admit that I am afraid, I will. If you want me to say I am bored, I will."

"I want you to tell me what happened! Eleanor, this is a huge problem," he answered.

"We need to know what happened so it doesn't happen to others. It's been six months. We have been patient. You are not a child, Eleanor. You are *seventeen* and next year you become a trainer yourself. Do you understand your responsibility, Eleanor?"

Eleanor, Eleanor, Eleanor!

Mr. Tarniby had moved very close and his voice had grown louder. I could smell cigars on his breath. His large face was even bigger this close up. But his eyes were still very, very small. The veins across his forehead were a deep, ugly blue.

"I am not going to train. I am not going to travel. I told you I can't remember what happened. I remember feeling weak. So tired. I remember my reflection. I don't know what I was looking into but I saw myself. My eyes were bloodshot and my hair was thin. My face was pale and sagging. I was dying," I answered.

I watched his face change and his shoulders slump. I always won when I played the death card. It was a low move on my part, but I had to get out of there.

He nodded his head and reached down beside my desk. When he stood, he was holding my red backpack for me. I slid my arms into the straps and walked quickly out of the room.

2

The air was soft and fresh on my face. I could smell the trees budding and a hint of rain in the air.

Mrs. Beils said that time travel makes a person more aware of their surroundings. Smells become stronger. Noises become louder. Colors become brighter. I guess that's true, but it's not a reward. Not when you consider what I had lost.

I shook my head again. I promised myself I would stop thinking about him. For all it mattered, he was dead. I would never see him again. I didn't even know what year he was from.

And if I did, it wouldn't matter, since I could never stay. Jumpers cant exist for long outside of their own time.

Before me, the longest known jump happened two generations ago. A man named Idan was gone for just over a year. His jump was planned to be no longer than three months.

But he fell in love. Unfortunately, the woman lived three hundred years in his past.

He came back only when his body was very close to dying. He was too weak to jump back to her and it drove him mad. We learned about it in class. Mrs. Beils felt sorry for him and was almost fired for saying so.

"You all understand, don't you?" the head trainer had yelled. "It's his fault and we should not feel bad. He broke two of our most important rules. You do not EVER disobey your return time. And you never, NEVER become personally involved." Then the head trainer had stomped out of the room, still angry. A very embarrassed Mrs. Beils was left to continue class.

Idan was imprisoned for attempting a jump without permission. He had shown signs of recovery the week before. He had decided it was the only way.

It turned out that he was not strong enough to jump alone. And he was too weak to move afterwards. They found him lying on his own broken legs. He had been in prison ever since. I must be a horrible person, because part of me wished that I were him. At least he got a chance to try. He *knew* where to find her and what to do. I wish for him that he had succeeded, but at least he got to try.

There would be no trying for me. It was not only illegal but impossible to jump forward.

At least it was... until I accidentally did it.

8

3

"Elli", he had whispered into my ear. "Wake Up."

I opened my eyes to see Chase sitting on the bed beside me. A quick peek at the window told me it was still night-time.

"What're you doing?" I asked, rubbing at my eyes as I sat up.

He smiled. "I have a surprise," he said. "Something they didn't have back in your day, old lady."

I giggled as I swung my feet to the floor. He helped me to slip on a pair of soft shoes and held his finger to his lips. "Shhh," he warned, opening the bedroom door.

We tiptoed down the dark hallway and quietly crept through the front door. I continued following him all the way down the perfectly smooth road. The sky was filled with the color of passing space vehicles.

Finally I asked, "Where are we going?"

"Just a little further," he answered. He pulled me down a winding path and I could hear water running. I looked down and saw a river moving beside us. "Right down there," he said, pointing his finger toward the water's edge.

We stepped carefully over large stones until the water was only inches away.

"It's beautiful," I said, giggling a little. "But we do have water where I come from."

I watched the way his blonde hair moved when he shook his head. "No," he said, his brown eyes staring down at me. "That's not the surprise."

He pulled a small red can from his back pocket and waved his arm. A mist of spray came rushing out of the can. He continued moving his arm up, down, circle, and over again.

When he stopped, I just looked at him, confused. "Take's a minute," he told me, feeling confident.

In the next moment, there were tiny lights moving quickly in our direction. They were coming from everywhere. As they grew closer, I realized they were tiny lightning bugs.

"They're attracted to the spray," Chase said. "It hangs in the air for a few minutes."

The insects flew nearer into the mist. They began flying close together, in a sort of pattern. It was beautiful. But then it got even better. In awe, I pulled my hand to my mouth and felt tears in my eyes. I looked at Chase and then at the light show once more. I stared for a few moments at the three little words spelled into the air in front of me.

Then I stood on my tiptoes and pressed a kiss to the base of Chase's jaw. "I love you too," I whispered.

Leap of Faith

4

I flopped down on the bed feeling lost, angry, and depressed. It had been six months since I returned to my own time and I had only been awake for four of them. Two of them were spent in intensive care recovering from my two year jump.

I pushed my hands through my curly hair and sat forward on my elbows.

Was Chase trying to get to me? I wondered. Had he moved on already? I mean, it's not like we were separated by a few blocks. Hell, there weren't even mountains or oceans between us. That would have been a piece of cake. But time? How do you mess with that? Even if I managed to get to him, I'd die. Like I almost did before.

I felt the tears beginning to form in my eyes. It was the same every night. I would eat a small dinner, if anything at all. I would head to bed early and think about how to find him. And I would cry until I fell asleep when I realized it was impossible. Every day ended the same way.

Not today, I thought. I pushed up from the bed and walked across the room. I glanced quickly at the mirror and frowned. I looked like crap.

Feeling sorry for myself was getting me nowhere. Crying was getting me nowhere. It was time for a new plan, I decided.

I pulled a small, yellow notebook from my desk and sat down. Opening to a clean page, I began to brainstorm.

I wrote down everything I knew about jumping. It can be done by one person, I wrote. But it is very difficult and very risky. And the only people who have ever tried ended up in prison. That's where most died. To my knowledge, there were five of them and only one was still alive.

I tapped my fingers against my forehead. What was his name? I remembered hearing about him in class. Percy? Was that it?

I pushed the green button on my computer. "Percy's Illegal Jump," I typed. Hundreds of images appeared. I was once again surprised by how young he looked.

"Percy Marving," I read, "a twenty-year old trainer, was found guilty today. He performed an illegal jump three months ago. He is recovering in Newburn Hospital. He will be relocated to Landers Prison when stable."

That was two years ago. I wrote the information into my notebook. "Percy Marving. Age 22. Landers Prison." I found the address and wrote this down also. Then I smiled, a plan forming in my mind. It was the first time I had smiled in what felt like years. Tomorrow, things might actually change.

Leap of Faith

5

The prison was just under thirty minutes away. I sat on the air trolley between two very large women. I wasn't sure if I would be allowed inside once I arrived. I wasn't sure if Percy was still being held there at all. But it was the only plan I had at the moment.

A loud bell rang and the lights turned on in the small vehicle. It lowered to the ground and my stop was announced over the speakers. I grabbed my backpack and a box of muffins and stepped outdoors.

In front of me was a very long brick building and a huge fence. I had read about fences in my textbook but had never seen one. No use fencing in someone who can time travel, after all.

And the jumper community was very snobby. Jumpers only. It was the one thing I hated at first. I hardly ever saw my family once I had decided to train.

I took a deep breath and walked to the entrance. The inside of the building was very white and very cold. There was one long hallway with several doors. A huge desk and a tiny older man with a mustache blocked my way to the hallway.

"Name?" he called to me.

"Eleanor," I answered. "Eleanor Pram."

"Appointment?" he asked next.

"No, I was hoping I could surprise someone," I said with a shaky voice.

"You want to see Percy?" he asked, looking up for the first time.

"Yes. How do you know?" I wondered aloud.

"Only inmate," he replied. That should have been obvious to me. There were very few arrests in the jumper community. People followed rules very carefully. The gift was not to be taken for granted.

I stood quietly for a moment as the tiny man wrote something down. "We don't usually allow visitors without an appointment," he said. "But, we are very quiet today. Wait here."

He walked down the hallway and out of sight. A minute later, a short young woman appeared. "You're here to see Percy?" she asked.

"Yes," I answered, smiling because this might really work.

She waved her hand and I followed her to the last door on the left. She opened it and led us into a tiny room. It was even whiter and colder in here. There was nothing but a large white table and two white folding chairs.

She asked me to have a seat and then she left.

Leap of Faith

It felt like hours before the door opened again. When it did, the tiny man was leading a young, tired looking prisoner through it. His wrists were handcuffed. His head was shaved and there was a small metal box above his left ear.

I instantly felt sick. I remembered reading about those. They pass currents through your brain. It blocks your ability to jump and is supposedly really painful.

I looked down at my hands as he took the other seat. The tiny man turned to me and pointed to a button on the desk. "If you need anything, press this," he said. And then he left.

Percy sat silently and stared at me. His look was not friendly nor unkind. He just seemed tired. So, so tired.

"I'm Eleanor," I told him nervously.

"Percy," he said, nodding to me.

He looked too thin in his huge blue shirt. I wondered when he had last eaten. I pushed the box of muffins towards him.

"I brought these for you," I said.

He just continued to sit and stare. I didn't know how to start. I twisted my hair awkwardly for a moment.

"I was hoping you could answer some questions," I said quietly.

He nodded his head, showing no emotion. "School project?" he asked.

"No, no," I told him. "I'm personally interested. If that's okay."

"Nothing better to do," he shrugged. "Shoot."

"How," I said, my voice shaking again. "How did you, you know. How did you jump alone?"

"That seems like a dangerous question," he warned. He sat up straighter and looked at me. He seemed to come alive all at once. "You wouldn't be trying it yourself, would you?" he asked. Then he smiled. A huge, bright smile.

"No, no, never," I stammered. "I just want to know. " I could tell that he didn't believe me and his smile grew larger.

"Don't care if you do," he said. "Just wondering."

I sat quietly, waiting for him to say more. Finally he did.

6

"Anyone can do it," he told me, his eyes twinkling. "They don't teach this, because it is dangerous. Not so much for you, but for them. If people start jumping whenever and wherever, they lose their power. It would be chaos."

I was stunned by his words. I could feel my palms sweating and my heart pounding.

Anyone can jump alone? It couldn't be true.

"But how?" I wondered. "Wouldn't people try?"

"If that's so, why haven't you?" he asked me.

"Um, well... it's too dangerous. Without being in the right environment, I mean. As long as there are doctors monitoring you, the risk is small. You must know this," I answered.

He rolled his eyes. "There is no risk. Not during the jump. Your *mind* grows weak from too much jumping but that's normal. The doctors can't stop that. Your body is fine though. You don't lose limbs. Bones don't break. Organs can't collapse. Not in the jump itself, anyway. Staying outside of your time too long is another story."

"But what about Idan?" I asked. "He broke his legs in a jump."

Percy's expression changed immediately. He looked suddenly serious and very, very angry.

"No," he said quietly. "They did that when they found him. His mind was too weak to make the jump. When they caught him, they made an example of him. They had to make it match their stories. They broke both of his legs as a warning to others."

I gasped loudly. It couldn't be true. I felt a cold chill run down my spine. It was such a kind, supportive community. A bit intense at times, but well-meaning. There was no way this could be true. I tried to calm my breathing and shook my head to clear the images away.

"If that's true, how do you jump?" I asked again.

"You concentrate. Harder and more deeply than you ever have in a jump bed. You don't need anyone to help you. You know where you are going. Visualize it. And let yourself fall," he said.

"But couldn't I get lost without them tracking me?" I asked, keeping my voice low. There were footsteps approaching in the hallway. Percy leaned forward over the table and whispered to me.

"No," he said slowly. "They want you to be afraid to jump without them. You can always come back. They tell you that to control you. The gift is too rare for them to risk losing it. They have plans for you, Eleanor. For all of us. And those don't include us traveling freely."

"Why did you come back?" I asked. I instantly felt embarrassed because it was none of my business.

He looked down at his hands and his shoulders sank. He suddenly appeared much older. "Coward," he answered. It sounded almost like he was calling himself the word.

"I don't understand," I told him.

"You think you are ready to die. It can't be worse than prison, right? Than being without her? I was ready to die with her. To die before I ever left her. But then death came. And it was so real. I didn't want to die, Eleanor. I'm a coward."

I felt tears stinging the corners of my eyes. "No," I told him, reaching out to cover his hand with my own. "You are not a coward. I'm sorry you lost her. I'm so sorry," I whispered.

I heard the keys sliding into the door. The tiny man must have come back for me. I stood and slipped my backpack over my shoulder.

"Thanks for your time," I said quietly before turning towards the door.

"Eleanor?" Percy called, startling me. I spun around to face him just before the door opened. "I hope you find him," he whispered. Then the tiny man led me away.

28

7

"Ellie!" Chase had yelled. "Wake up!" He pulled the pillow from beneath my head and hit me lightly. "Wake up, Santa came!" he laughed.

I groaned and rolled away from him. I looked out the window. Still dark. Why couldn't he ever let me sleep at least until the sun came up?

He held out a glass of water and some pancakes. "Come on, Ellie! Presents!" he urged.

Leap of Faith

He pulled the blankets down and I shivered. "Are they going anywhere?" I asked sleepily. "If not, can't I see them in an hour? Or maybe five?"

He rolled his eyes. "I don't think so. Up!"

I pushed onto my elbows stiffly and grabbed for the sweatshirt lying on my bed.

I knew it would do no good to protest. I followed him down to the living room. A huge tree was decorated in the corner. There was garland hanging along the walls and soft music playing. A fire was burning and the windows were sprayed with fake snow.

"I thought you don't make a big deal of Christmas?" I asked, looking around. It felt so cozy and so welcoming in the small space.

"I don't," he replied, "but since you can't remember ever celebrating one..."

I smiled wide and shook my head. "You shouldn't have," I told him.

He blushed lightly and looked away toward the tree. There were three presents resting beneath it.

"Those are for you," he said, pointing. I felt a rush of excitement. Jumpers do not celebrate Christmas. They don't celebrate holidays at all. I asked Chase to wait for me while I ran back to my room. I pulled a small blue package from beneath the bed. Then I returned and sat beneath the tree. He sat beside me.

"You first," I said, placing the box in his hands.

"You shouldn't have gotten me anything, El," he said in a stern voice.

"Why, because you don't deserve presents? I live in your home. I eat your food. I learn from you. You've given everything to me in the past year. And I love you. Plus, it's really small. Open it."

"You don't owe me anything and *I'm* supposed to take care of *you*. I'm older," he winked. He found it funny that he had five more years of life than I did. Since I was from his past, I was technically born first.

"Just open it," I said as I rolled my eyes.

He tore quickly at the blue paper. Then he opened the box inside. I tried to read his expression. At first he seemed to have none.

Then he looked up at me. "Ellie," he said, a sadness coming over him. For a moment, I felt terrible. I hadn't meant to upset him.

"What's the matter?" I asked, feeling disappointed. He shook his head.

"It's perfect," he answered. He moved closer to me and wrapped an arm around my shoulder. He brushed my hair back from my face and gave me a kiss. "It's perfect," he said again.

We both looked down at the framed photo. In it, we were standing together in the park where we had met. We were holding hands and had our heads tilted into the sun.

"I don't want you to be just a photograph, El," he whispered. He pulled my head onto his shoulder and looked up at the tree. "We have to find a way."

"We will," I told him. I wiped my eyes quickly before he could see the tears that were ready to fall.

8

I lay on my bed, staring up at the same white ceiling. I could feel fear in my belly. It felt like a big burrito after you've been having salad for weeks.

I smiled at the comparison. At least I was slowly turning back into myself. I had no idea if this was going to work, but it gave me something to do.

I didn't need to cry anymore. I didn't need to miss Chase. I didn't need to wish that I had never been able to jump. I was going back to him.

It had been one week since I met Percy at Landers. I had spent six days doing research on my own. I practically lived at the local library. Except for my sessions with Mr. Tarniby. And even then, I was different. I smiled. I joked. I told Mr. Tarniby that I was thinking about starting my training again. That was probably a bit much but, man, you should have seen the look on his face.

I smiled at the memory. There was really nothing left to do but jump.

I felt sweat beading on my forehead and my hands shaking. I decided to concentrate on my breathing. I closed my eyes and felt my chest expand and contract.

In... and out. In... and out. One more in... and out.

My heart rate slowed and I felt more in control.

I kept my eyes closed and thought of the park. I thought of jumping there the first time, so far from where I was supposed to go. I thought of the loud cracking sounds as I ripped through time. I thought of the tree that

I fell from as I arrived. I thought of Chase's stunned face as I crashed down in the middle of his picnic date.

I laughed out loud. What a way to meet someone. His date was not amused.

Concentrate! I thought to myself, becoming serious once again. I imagined the apartment where I stayed with him. I imagined the office where he worked. I imagined the photograph of us, over and over again.

Suddenly, I felt a sharp familiar pull on my body. I opened my eyes and saw my bedroom fading. A darkness came flooding in.

Where I normally felt excitement, I felt fear. Cold, hard, unreasonable fear. I screamed and pulled back, falling hard onto the bed.

What if Percy was wrong? What if we couldn't all perform our own jumps? What if I ended up like Idan? Nothing more than a pile of broken bones in a prison cell.

I felt the tears building in my eyes and I swallowed hard. No. I was *not* crying. I had already decided.

I said that I wanted the chance to try. Whatever happened, I was taking that chance. It would be worth it. I needed to know that I had tried everything that I could.

I turned to my side and pulled the blankets up to my chin. I was exhausted from the short attempt. There is always tomorrow, I thought, as I quickly drifted off into a deep sleep.

9

Chase held my hand as I screamed. I felt my body being pulled back to its own time. I had no idea how they found me. No idea what to do.

I turned to him. I could tell that he was trying to hold back tears. His hands were shaking and his face was bright red.

"We knew you'd have to go, baby," he said. "Let them pull you back. I'll find you."

There was another sharp pain as I fought being torn away.

"We decided already!" I yelled to him. "If I can fight just a little longer, they'll think I am probably too weak to jump. They will give up, figuring I will die anyway."

His eyebrows moved down and he was suddenly very angry. "*We* didn't decide anything, Eleanor, you did!" he yelled.

My eyes snapped open and I looked up at him. He hardly ever used my full name anymore.

"*You* decided it would be easier to die than to go back without me. I never wanted that. It's selfish, El. What am I supposed to do when you're gone? Think about how loving me *killed* you?" he said. He started to cry openly, and I could no longer hold back my own tears.

"I'm not dying," I said shakily. I knew it was a lie.

My breathing had become difficult, and I hadn't been able to walk for a few days. Time was finally taking its toll on me. I had convinced myself that dying would be easier than going back and living in my own time alone. But then they found me.

I could hear their voices.... Mr. Tarniby, Mrs. Beils, and the rest of them working to bring me home. They were concentrating so hard that I was fading in and out of time and space.

Chase ignored my lie and held my hand tighter. He pressed a kiss to my mouth, and one of his tears fell onto my cheek. "I'll find you, baby," he whispered. "I wouldn't break a promise to you. Just go. I'll be with you soon."

There was suddenly so much darkness and so much pain. It may have been my weak body being pulled through hundreds of years. But I'm pretty sure it was my heart breaking.

Leap of Faith

10

I opened my eyes quickly as someone touched my leg. Bright lights beamed down on me, and I squinted to see. I was laying on a bed in a tiny room. A woman dressed in all white was wrapping my knees.

"What's going on?" I asked. I felt nervousness building in my belly. I hated not knowing where I was.

The woman did not look up until she had finished with my bandages. *Where are my clothes?* I wondered. *Did they find me already? Am I home?* Suddenly, panic gripped me and I fought to sit up.

The woman held my arms down and made a face. "That won't do you any good," she said in a strange accent. "You aren't quite ready to move yet."

I relaxed somewhat and stared at her. She looked at me and continued talking.

"Some children found you near the trees. Not sure what you were doing. A walk, maybe? Anyway, it seems that you passed out. You were unconscious when we got the call. That was yesterday. We have been patching you up since."

She looked over my bandaged body like it was a work of art. Her art. She smiled proudly.

"You should be up and about in no time," she said, still smiling.

"Where am I?" I asked her, feeling confused.

"My dear child, I just told you. We're fixing you up, so clearly you're in the hospital!" she answered.

"But what time? What is the year?" I asked again.

"Dear me!" she cried. "You must have really hit that head of yours! I'll get the doctor!" And she rushed out of the room with a look as nervous as I felt.

I gazed around me, looking for clues. The window was pulled shut. There were no devices to help me guess. A television would have been nice. I've always been good at guessing a year by the television model.

The only hint was the small screen beeping to my right. It was tiny and built into the top of my bed. It was clearly monitoring something.

My breathing? My heart rate? I wasn't sure.

A few minutes later a doctor stepped into the room. He too was wearing all white. He was much older than the woman before him and much calmer.

"Good to see you are awake," he said to me, holding out his hand. I gripped his palm and shook.

"Thanks," I muttered. "And can you tell me where I am?"

"You are in the J.D. Briggens hospital. In the emergency wing. Today is the second day of spring in the fortieth year."

"The fortieth year?" I asked.

"We don't want you to be alarmed. It seems you suffered some memory loss but only for a short time. We believe you will be back to normal within 48 hours. You just need to rest."

The fortieth year? I wondered to myself. What could that even mean? Did they change the way they organized time?

I began to laugh uncontrollably. Of all the things that could go wrong, I did not expect this. Not that it mattered. Chase and I never talked about time. We were frightened of it. It was the one thing that could pull us apart. I wouldn't know if this was his time even if I understood what the fortieth year was.

The doctor looked at me strangely. "May I ask what's funny?" he said politely.

"Just nervous," I said. He then asked me if I had any questions and I said no. Soon I was alone in the room again. I kicked my legs out and winced. It was painful but they could move.

I needed to get out of here, I decided. I needed to see if Chase was here.

I slid off the bed carefully and found my clothes in a nearby chair. I removed the hospital gown and pulled my dirty jeans on. Throwing my shirt over my head, I stepped toward the door.

The hallway was empty so I opened the door quietly and closed it behind me. I carried my shoes so that I could move without being heard. I walked down the hall, looking for a map. Or an exit sign. Anything to help me get out of there. A plaque on the wall pointed to the main lobby.

I followed it.

Just as I turned the corner into a large room, an alarm sounded. I crouched automatically and looked around. I

Leap of Faith

expected them to wonder where I went, but I didn't expect this. *Am I a prisoner?* I wondered.

Two doors opened from the outside, and I realized the alarm was not for me. It was signalling an incoming patient. *How stupid of me.* I breathed a sigh of relief and stood up straight. The exit was right there. I stepped forward, ignoring the man at the front desk.

I walked quickly and quietly ahead, not making eye contact with anyone. I was right next to the door. I waited for two large men to push a rolling bed into the room.

Just as I brushed past them, I looked down at the new patient. He was covered in a sheet but his arms hung at his sides. They were covered in bruises. One appeared to be bent at an odd angle. I bent my head, ashamed that I had looked and sorry for his pain. I was just opening the door to leave when I heard my name. I spun around and looked back at the patient. I felt my heart pound in my chest.

A pair of eyes in a too-thin face with dirty skin looked up at me. I felt my body pulled forward and my face was wet with tears.

"Chase," I mumbled, taking his hand. "How are you...why are you...what happened?" I asked.

He was clearly in pain but he smiled through it. "I found you Ellie," he said. He squeezed my hand just as his body began to shake. His eyes rolled backward and he shook harder.

"What's happening?" I screamed, turning to the people beside me. "Do something!"

I tried to hold onto his hand but I was pulled away. A pair of arms pushed me into a nearby chair while I continued to yell.

Three men in blue wheeled Chase quickly down the hall. They yelled orders just as they rounded the corner.

Soon I couldn't hear them anymore. I couldn't see them anymore. Everything blurred together into a mess of colors and sounds. I might have still been yelling. I wasn't sure. The only thing that I was sure of was that something was very, very wrong.

Leap of Faith

11

Today was the day. It had now been two weeks since I met Percy. Plenty of time to become completely wrapped up in my own fear. And I was terrified. After all, I had been told my entire life about the dangers of jumping alone.

Prison didn't seem so bad. Not when exploded organs and broken bones were a possibility.

Leap of Faith

I walked out of my tiny apartment and headed down the road. I looked at the buildings that lined the street. They were all the same, with more apartments like mine.

I saw two children sitting under a tree sharing a book. Their wide eyes were the same shape and the same blue. They had the same blonde hair and the same crooked nose. Siblings.

It was rare for two family members to be jumpers, though no one knew why.

I realized that I was jealous of them. At least they had each other here.

I walked a little farther and looked up as one of the air buses passed overhead. I wondered who they were and where they were going. Then I realized it didn't matter.

I kept moving until I reached the edge of the pavement. The only thing ahead of me was a thick forest. I looked around to see if anyone was watching. It wasn't against the rules to enter, but it was definitely weird. Jumper students hardly ever had time to do anything besides train. That meant lots of reading, lots of exams, more reading, and sleeping whenever possible. It did not mean exploring nature.

The coast was clear, so I stepped into the patch of trees. I didn't know where I was going, only that I needed to keep moving. I couldn't go back to my room. I wouldn't be able to jump.

I couldn't watch the children reading in the grass. I wouldn't be able to jump. No, I had to get away from what was familiar to me. I needed to be unafraid of losing this life.

I came up to a huge rock at the edge of a pond. I dug my shoes into its side and climbed up carefully. The top was smooth and flat. A perfect bed.

I leaned back and rested my head against the cold stone. Then I began to breathe. In, and out. A huge breath in, and a deep breath out. Slowly I felt myself relaxing.

When I finally felt in control of myself and my fear, I pictured Chase. I pictured his face and the way he smiled. I pictured his arms around me. I pictured our first kiss and our first Christmas.

I focused on all of the little details. His eye color. His skin tone. His freckles. His large, clumsy hands. Soon it felt like he was right there with me.

That is when I began to picture places. I imagined meeting his parents at the library. I imagined the restaurant where we had our first real date.

I imagined the river where he told me he loved me.

I began to feel so warm and so happy. I could almost feel his hand in mine as I thought about it. I could almost feel the water on my feet.

I even heard his voice in my head, as if he were speaking to me right then. A blackness soon surrounded me. I closed my eyes and continued to relax. I imagined that he was calling my name.

The blackness crept closer. I felt heavy at first, but then completely weightless.

It was almost like dropping into a pool and floating to the top. I lost track of time and place and even myself.

Then the spinning started. I felt like I was being dropped head over feet again and again. It was a surprisingly good feeling. I was tumbling lightly, like waves were rocking me.

I knew better than to open my eyes. I kept them shut tightly and soon I felt heavy once more. Weight returned to my body and I was falling quickly. There was a bright flash and a loud cracking sound. My back fell against something solid and I couldn't breath. I rolled onto my side, coughing and trying to find air. It felt likes hours before I found a breath. I inhaled deeply and opened my eyes. Every part of my body ached. I noticed a large cut in my left arm and my jaw felt swollen.

I cringed as I stood to look around. I was so sore. I shook my arms and legs to try to loosen up.

In front of me was a group of trees, much like the one I had just left. On either side of me were a bunch of buildings.

They were all different shapes and sizes. They were clearly not a part of my jumper community. But I didn't recognize where they could be, and I felt my stomach sink.

Please, please tell me that I jumped to the right time. Please tell me that this is where Chase is. I felt tears pooling in my eyes. *Please be here.*

Leap of Faith

12

I don't know how long I sat there, just waiting. Waiting for a doctor. Waiting for news. Waiting to understand anything about what was happening.

Finally, a short woman stepped into the lobby and called my name. I jumped to my feet and walked toward her.

"You're Eleanor?" she asked again. I nodded.

Leap of Faith

"Alright, come with me please."

We walked together down the same hallway as earlier. At the end, she swiped a card through a door handle. It opened wide and I followed her through.

"How is Chase?" I asked. I couldn't wait any longer to find out.

"He's stable," she answered and kept walking. Something about her short answer worried me. I followed her down another hall. The door numbers increased as we moved. We finally stopped just outside of room 31A. She motioned for me to walk ahead of her.

I stepped into the room and saw Chase. He was lying with his head turned away from the door. There were several IV's hooked into his arms and he looked pale. Too pale. I inched closer.

He turned his face toward mine and I watched his eyes light up. He looked like he was about to yell to me. His voice came out in a whisper instead.

"Come here, baby," he said, patting the bed beside him. He pushed himself into a sitting position. I stepped toward him, shaking somewhat. I eased my legs up beside him and folded into his arms. Then I began to cry.

"I missed you so much," I sobbed into his shoulder. He pulled me closer. The woman looked like she was about to speak. Instead she backed out of the room and left.

"I missed you too," he whispered into my hair. He kissed my forehead and I looked up, still crying.

"Where are we?" I asked him after my sobbing stopped.

"I was hoping to ask you that," he answered, suddenly serious.

"You don't know?"

"Well I jumped to *your* time," I told him.

"No, I jumped to yours," he corrected me.

"That's impossible," I said. I straightened up in bed and stared at him. "You can't jump."

"You forget where I come from, El. In my time, jumping is no longer genetic. They've been working to perfect it for some time now. I signed up as a trial jumper. I'm like a robo-you." He smirked at me. "Though obviously not as skilled," he added, waving at his injuries.

His eyes turned to my own bandaged legs and the small cuts on my face. "Although, it looks like you had a rough time too. Are you okay?" he asked. His soft voice made me cry a second time.

"So what does this mean?" I asked, ignoring his question. My sobbing continued. I slid my hand into his and leaned against his shoulder. "Where are we?"

"My best guess," he said, "is that we didn't jump to a certain time. I don't know if it's possible, but I think we might have jumped to each other."

"You mean we can find one another without a specific time? We don't need to picture an actual place?"

"That's what I did," he replied. "I have never been to your time, remember? When they hooked me up to their equipment, they gave me directions. They told me what to imagine. They were sending me back, far back. I think to test our limits, maybe. I pretended to do what they asked but I thought of you instead. I thought of your face and your hair. Over and over."

My crying was now intense. I could not believe that he had found me. I couldn't believe that this perfect boy would risk so much for me.

We sat in silence for a few minutes. I listened to his breathing. I looked at his hand, curled into my own. After so much pain and so much waiting, I finally felt at home.

13

"Happy anniversary, baby," Chase said, resting a small cake on the table. There were three candles sticking out of it. One for each year that we had been together again. I looked up at him.

He still had a young face, though there were now deep creases by his eyes. His blonde hair was sprinkled with gray, like my own. I was still only twenty-two and he was now twenty-seven. For anyone else, that would have been young. For us, time was already taking a toll.

I smiled as I blew at the three small flames. "There should really be six candles here," I told him. "I met you six years ago."

"We weren't married then, silly," he answered, pulling my chin up with his hand. He leaned down and kissed me softly. "So it doesn't count."

I laughed, remembering. I had been only fifteen when I had first met Chase.

We had two amazing years together before I was pulled back to my own time. Those six months that we had spent searching for one another were the longest of our lives. But we did it.

"What's next, baby?" Chase asked. I shook my head to clear my thoughts and looked at him once more. "Next we eat it," I answered, pointing to the cake. He laughed and sat himself in the chair beside me.

"You know what I mean," he said. He leaned forward and cut two slices from the cake.

"I guess we hope for an even better year," I told him. I swiped at the frosting with my finger. "This is delicious," I added.

He looked at me carefully, the way he had on our past two anniversaries. There was a mix of love, hope, and fear in his eyes. It was the same mix of feelings that I felt inside me.

"There's always a chance they'll find a solution," he said.

I heard a familiar sadness in his voice. He was always wishing that there would be more time.

"We just have to enjoy right now and I guess wait and see," I answered. I understood his desire for a normal life. I wish that we had been born into the same time. I wish that I didn't see time wearing away at us day by day.

"I just don't want us to fade away too quickly," he said. "I have so much more I need to do with you."

I felt tears running from my eyes. They weren't the sad kind, though. They're the kind that fall when you love someone that much.

I swiped my finger through the frosting once more. I leaned close and dabbed a dot of it on his nose and smiled.

"We won't ever fade away," I told him.

"We found each other, somehow. We were centuries apart and we found each other. If time can't stop this," I said, holding up my wedding ring, "nothing can. Whatever comes next, we're in it together."

He took my face in his hands once more and lifted my chin. His blue eyes looked straight into my own for a moment before he kissed me. It was the kind of kiss that you give just in case. Just in case tomorrow doesn't come. Just in case this stops being real. Just in case you don't get another chance. I felt his tears mixing with my own on our faces. I felt his arms holding me. And I kissed him back, with all the love I had inside of me. I kissed him just in case.

About The Author

Angela Dellisola lives in Massachusetts with her husband, 2 dogs, 3 cats, and 20,000+ honeybees. Her story "Leap of Faith" was the 2015 People's Choice Winner of the first Storyshares annual writing contest. She is now the Content Manager for the organization and loves being on the receiving end of all the great books filling their library's shelves.

Leap of Faith

About The Publisher

Story Shares is a nonprofit focused on supporting the millions of teens and adults who struggle with reading by creating a new shelf in the library specifically for them. The ever-growing collection features content that is compelling and culturally relevant for teens and adults, yet still readable at a range of lower reading levels.

Story Shares generates content by engaging deeply with writers, bringing together a community to create this new kind of book. With more intriguing and approachable stories to choose from, the teens and adults who have fallen behind are improving their skills and beginning to discover the joy of reading. For more information, visit storyshares.org.

Easy to Read. Hard to Put Down.